Tip-Tap Pop

by
Sarah Lynn

illustrated by
Valeria Docampo

Marshall Cavendish Children

Marshall Cavendish Corporation
99 White Plains Road, Tarrytown, NY 10591
www.marshallcavendish.us/kids

The illustrations were rendered
in gouache and pencils on paper.
Book design by Vera Soki
Editor: Marilyn Brigham

Printed in Malaysia (T)
First edition
1 3 5 6 4 2

mc Marshall Cavendish
Children

Library of Congress Cataloging-in-Publication Data

Lynn, Sarah, 1975–
Tip-tap pop / Sarah Lynn, [illustrations by] Valeria
Docampo. — 1st ed.
p. cm.
Summary: Emma and Pop have been tap dancing
together since before she could talk, but Pop becomes
very forgetful and can no longer dance until one
special day when he hears Emma's steps and they
find a way for him to join in.
ISBN 978-0-7614-5712-1
[1. Tap dancing—Fiction. 2. Grandfathers—Fiction.
3. Memory—Fiction.]
I. Docampo, Valeria, 1976– ill. II. Title.
PZ7.L995252
[E]—dc22
2009029344

To my grandparents, my parents, my husband, my children,
and to the strength of the bond that links us all together
—S. L.

For my grandfathers, Herman and Joaquim.
For Grandma Perla, Loli, and Mingo, who are still dancing
—V. D.

Pop taught Emma to tap before she could talk.
Clickety-clack, clickety-clack,
buffalo-step-stomp.

"Music is everywhere," he whispered, pulling her close. "I will show you how to make it with your feet."

They **back-flapped** at the farmer's market,
past strawberries and kettle corn,
and **dig-shuffle-chugged**
through town.

And every year on Emma's birthday,
Pop and Emma put on a

clickety-clacking,

tip-tapping show . . .

... until the smell of Gram's famous strawberry shortcake made their noses tingle and their mouths water.

Then Pop and Emma would puff up their cheeks and blow out her candles together.

But one year, as summer Popsicles melted down
sticky fingers, slowly . . . Pop stopped dancing.
Soon, Pop forgot his reading glasses.
He forgot to walk the dog.

He even forgot Emma's birthday.
So Emma shuffle-hop-clacked
and blew out her candles.
Alone.

And then . . .

Pop forgot Gram's flour-caked hands.
He forgot Emma's **tip-tap-tapping**.
Pop sat quietly in his rocking chair,
the dog at his feet,
all day long.

Gram walked Emma to dance class.
Emma's shoes went **clunk stomp thud**,
as if her feet were made of bricks.
Her legs felt too heavy to dance.

Other **shuffle-hopping** feet
dig-chug-chugged across the floor.
Emma tried to listen to their music,
but all she heard was noise.

After class, Emma **clomped** over to Pop,
pressing her lips to his scratchy cheek.
A smile danced in his eyes,
then it melted away.

Emma's tap shoes **click-clacked** across Gram's porch. **Heel-toe-ball-heel.**

From behind her, Pop's slippers whispered. **Shuff-shuffle-rustle-slide.**

Emma whirled around. "Pop, you remember how to dance!" **Brush-brush-heel-heel**, her feet encouraged.

Pop's lips moved
but made no sound.
Then,
swoosh-swoosh-chug-chug,
he answered with his feet.

Emma wrapped her arms around him.
A slow smile spread
from her lips
to her cheeks
to her eyes.

Emma climbed the attic stairs and
dug out Pop's old tap shoes,
white and dusty, but still a perfect fit.

All afternoon they danced.
Pop **shuff-shuffled** his feet,
while Emma **buffalo-stepped**
around him,
until Pop sat down
to rest.

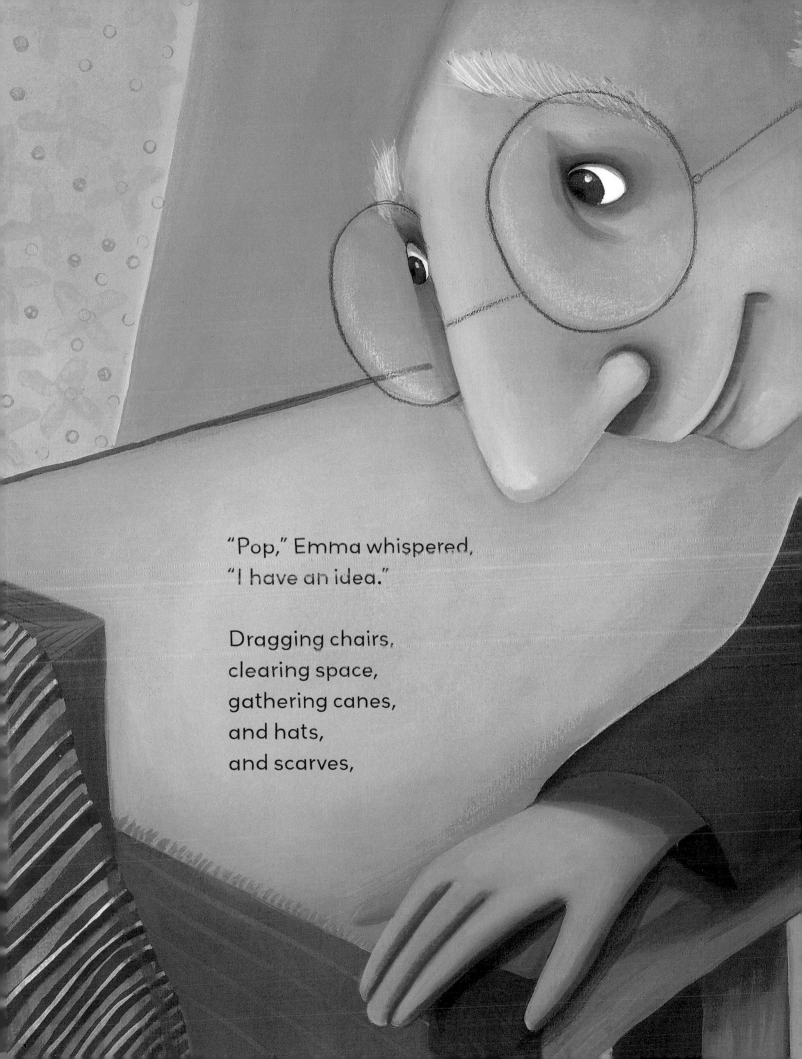

"Pop," Emma whispered,
"I have an idea."

Dragging chairs,
clearing space,
gathering canes,
and hats,
and scarves,

Emma put on a
clickety-clacking,
tip-tapping show
for the whole family.

Pop watched from a chair,
his feet **shuffling**
as the dog licked Pop's fingers
and *wag-wagged* his tail.

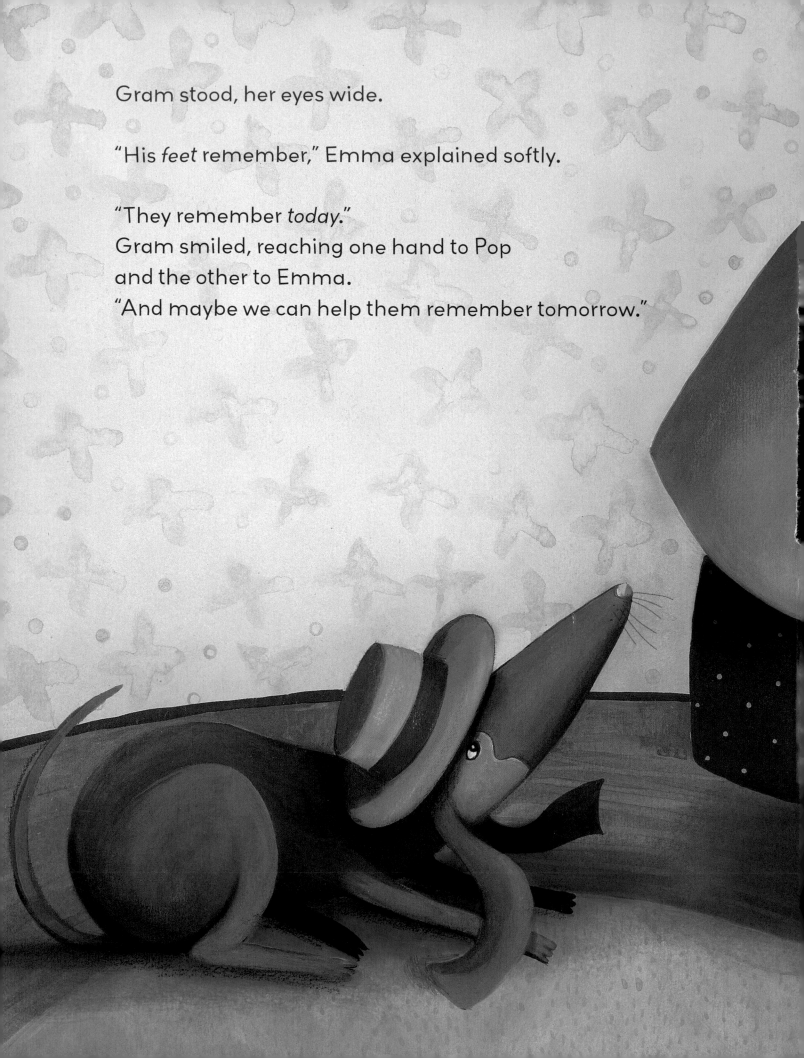

Gram stood, her eyes wide.

"His *feet* remember," Emma explained softly.

"They remember *today*."
Gram smiled, reaching one hand to Pop
and the other to Emma.
"And maybe we can help them remember tomorrow."

Stomp-stomp-clickety-clack,
clickety-clack, clickety-clack,
stomp-stomp-clickety-clack . . .
clickety-clack . . .

Together they slowly
tip-tapped down the street.
And Emma knew she'd always
remember the music of their feet.